Billy

Colleen Alton

AUSTIN MACAULEY PUBLISHERS™

LONDON ★ CAMBRIDGE ★ NEW YORK ★ SHARJAH

A CIP catalogue record for this title is available from the British Library.

ISBN 9781788781862 (Paperback)
ISBN 9781788781879 (ePub e-book)

www.austinmacauley.com

First Published 2022
Austin Macauley Publishers Ltd®
1 Canada Square
Canary Wharf
London
E14 5AA

About the Author

Colleen lives in East Sussex with her partner. Her children are now grown up, but when they were young, she created bedtime stories for them. Billy was their favourite and is the first one to be published.

For Isabelle and George

Jerry the bin man heard a whimper in the dustbin. "Stop!" he said to his workmate, "I think there's something alive in there."

He put his big orange gloved hands into the bin and pulled out a scraggy, dirty little dog.

"Poor thing," said Jerry to his mate.

"He looks unwell," he replied. "There's a vet round the corner, let's pop in and see if they can help."

"Don't worry now, boy, you're going to be OK," said Jerry to the dog as he cuddled him in the front of the bin cart. The dog was trembling, the man's hands were very big and he'd never been in a bin cart before, it was noisy.

The vet's room was very bright and clean.
"Poor thing, he's underfed," said the vet. "Leave him with me, I will take care of him, but what should we call him?"
"Billy!" blurted out Jerry, "I think he looks like a Billy!"

Two weeks later Jerry went back to see how Billy was doing. Jerry didn't recognise Billy, he was too lively, healthy and happy to be the scruffy little mutt he had brought in. He felt a little sad, he wanted to take Billy home, but his wife was allergic to pets.

The Dog Warden arrived, Jerry gave Billy a cuddle and reluctantly handed him over to the Dog Warden.

"I hope you find a good home for him," said Jerry.

"We will do our very best," said the Dog Warden.

Billy was scared, where was he going to end up now. "There now, Billy, we will look after you until someone comes to give you a proper home," said the Dog Warden.

Over the weeks Billy made lots of friends with the other dogs. There was Racy, a greyhound who had run out of steam and Cinders the soppy Cocker Spaniel, but his best friend was Rufus, a very shaggy dog who Billy loved because he was such fun to play with.

Each afternoon the dog pound would open to visitors, people who wanted to give one of the dogs a home, but for some reason no one ever stopped to look at Billy.
It was a Sunday when he saw Racy being adopted by a couple. Racy looked radiant as she was chosen, Billy would miss her but was so pleased that she had found owners to love her.
Days passed and Billy, Cinders and Rufus continued to play.

On a rainy day two smartly dressed men came by and spent a lot of time with Cinders. Cinders desperately wanted a family and Billy was delighted for her when he saw her having a smart collar and lead put on. He would miss her though.
There were other dogs to play with, but Billy still loved his best friend Rufus the most.

On a sunny Friday afternoon, a family arrived, they spent some time looking at Billy. *This is good,* he thought, *very good. I may have a family to love me.* He made himself look as smart as possible, but they left taking no one.

Next week the family came back, they smiled at Billy, but adopted Rufus. Billy was heartbroken. He hadn't been chosen and had lost his best friend. Billy smiled at his friend, he did not want him to feel sad that he had been chosen instead of him. They looked and nodded at each other as they passed.

The days passed slowly after that. The wardens were worried about Billy, he was obviously sad.
It was nearly closing time on Sunday, a little old lady arrived in a rather shabby raincoat.
Billy was feeling lonely.

"Who's been here the longest?" she said to the Dog Warden.
"That will be Billy; very sad, found abandoned in a bin, been here for quite a while now," replied the Dog Warden.
Billy hoped that the old lady would choose him. He didn't mind where he lived so long as he was loved and cared for.

"I'll take him," she said.
"Well," said the Dog Warden, "there are lots of papers to fill in."
"Mmmm," said the old lady. "Let's go to your office."

The old lady returned, with a worn collar and a piece of string, took Billy and shook the Dog Warden's hand.

Billy walked down the road with the old lady and they went underground. This was new to Billy, he was afraid, but the old lady talked to him all the time. "Don't worry, Billy, we are going on a train underground, it's called 'The Tube', it will be fun."
On the Tube she sat him on her lap and he looked at all the other people.

"Now, Billy, we are going on a bus, nothing to worry about, you're with me," said the old lady.
Billy felt good, the old lady was kind, and was stroking his ear.

They got off the bus. It was very busy with lots of people about.
They began to walk down a very long wide road.
There was a park on the left and big buildings on the right.
They were walking towards a very large, very grand building.

The old lady walked up to the guard in his smart red uniform
and tall black furry hat. He saluted her and opened the gate.

"Good evening, ma'am," said a very smartly dressed gentleman.
"Good evening," she replied. "We have a new addition to our family, let me introduce Billy to you."

The old lady took off her shabby raincoat and Billy finally realised who she was, THE QUEEN. "Please have a bed made up for Billy next to mine, I want to settle him in."

Later that night, Billy was settled in his bed at the bottom of the Queen's bed. Billy had the best billet of all!

Later that year on Christmas Day, Jerry and his wife were watching the Queen's Speech on TV, Jerry couldn't believe his eyes, there was Billy with THE QUEEN! He was so happy to see Billy had found a home!